This book belongs to:

_____

I'd like to share a raspa with:

_____

Text Copyright © 2022 by Eliza M Garza
Illustrations Copyright © 2022 by Edna Galván

All rights reserved. Published by Amazon KDP. No part of this book may be reproduced or transmitted in any form or by any means, electronic or mechanical, including photocopying, recording, or by any information storage and retrieval system, without written permission from the publisher, except as permitted by U.S. copyright law.

For permissions, please contact: [authorelizamgarza@gmail.com]

First Edition, October 2022

The art was created and colored digitally.

"Special thanks to my parents, Leticia Contreras and Carlos Garza. Your great love and faithful prayers have moved mountains in my life. Thank you for believing in me and telling me that I could do anything. I believed you.

Thank you to Claudette M. Renteria for helping me launch this book. You are a helping hand and a bright light in my life. I am grateful for you."

ISBN: 979-8-3573787-6-7

RASPAS CON MI GRANDPA

A Spanglish story

By: Eliza M. Garza

Illustrated by: Edna Galván

Edited by: Chris Ardis

Snow Cones With My Grandpa

This book is dedicated to my grandparents, who turned their obstacles into stepping stones for my future, their struggles into wisdom for my heart, and their sacrifices into love for generations to come.

This book is especially dedicated to my Grandpa Chávez, who I love with all my being and miss terribly. Thank you for always being the first car in the pick-up line, Grandpa. I promise to honor you and carry your great love within me always.

And to Carlitos and Reign, my heart loves you more than you'll ever know.

I can hardly wait for the school bell to ring!

My teacher, Mrs. Contreras, says I have ants in my pants because I can hardly keep myself from squirming out of my seat.

"Y aquí tiene su raspa de tamarindo con limón, Señor Chávez. Muchas gracias por venir. ¡Hasta la próxima!"

("Here is your tamarind snow cone with lime, Mr. Chávez. Thank you for coming. Until next time!") Lupita says.

Here comes my favorite part-- watching her create the RAINBOW on my raspa!

I see her reach for the mango syrup and look on as she creates a thick, yellow stripe down the center.

She grabs the blue raspberry syrup and paints a beautiful bright blue on the left side of the raspa. I notice that the blue syrup bleeds into the yellow and creates a hint of green!

I can hardly contain myself as I see her finish it off with the red cherry syrup on the opposite side of the raspa.

She then takes a funnel and fills it with ice to create the dome shape on top of the raspa.

Next, she takes a long, thin stick and pokes three holes into the raspa.

She does this to make sure the syrup poured on top can travel all the way down the cup. This is important, so your raspa will not be dry on the bottom and you can sip on it while you scoop all of the delicious toppings!

"Coming right up!" says Lupita.

She gets started on my raspa and asks her helper, Genaro, to make my grandfather's raspa.

The raspa machines rumble loudly as Lupita and Genaro use them to shave the ice.

I tippy toe up and peek my head over the order window where Lupita is stationed.

I like how the ice looks like snow as it dispenses out of the ice chute into a white styrofoam cup that reads "Raspa King."

"¿Y para usted, Señor Chávez?"
"And for you, Mr. Chávez?"

"Una raspa sabor tamarindo con limón y chamoy."
("A tamarind-flavored snow cone with lime and chamoy.")

TAMARINDO

Tamarind is a plump, pod-like fruit that grows on the tamarind tree, which is found in tropical areas such as Africa, India, and some parts of Asia. It is known for having a sweet and sour taste. It is a popular flavor and candy in South Texas.

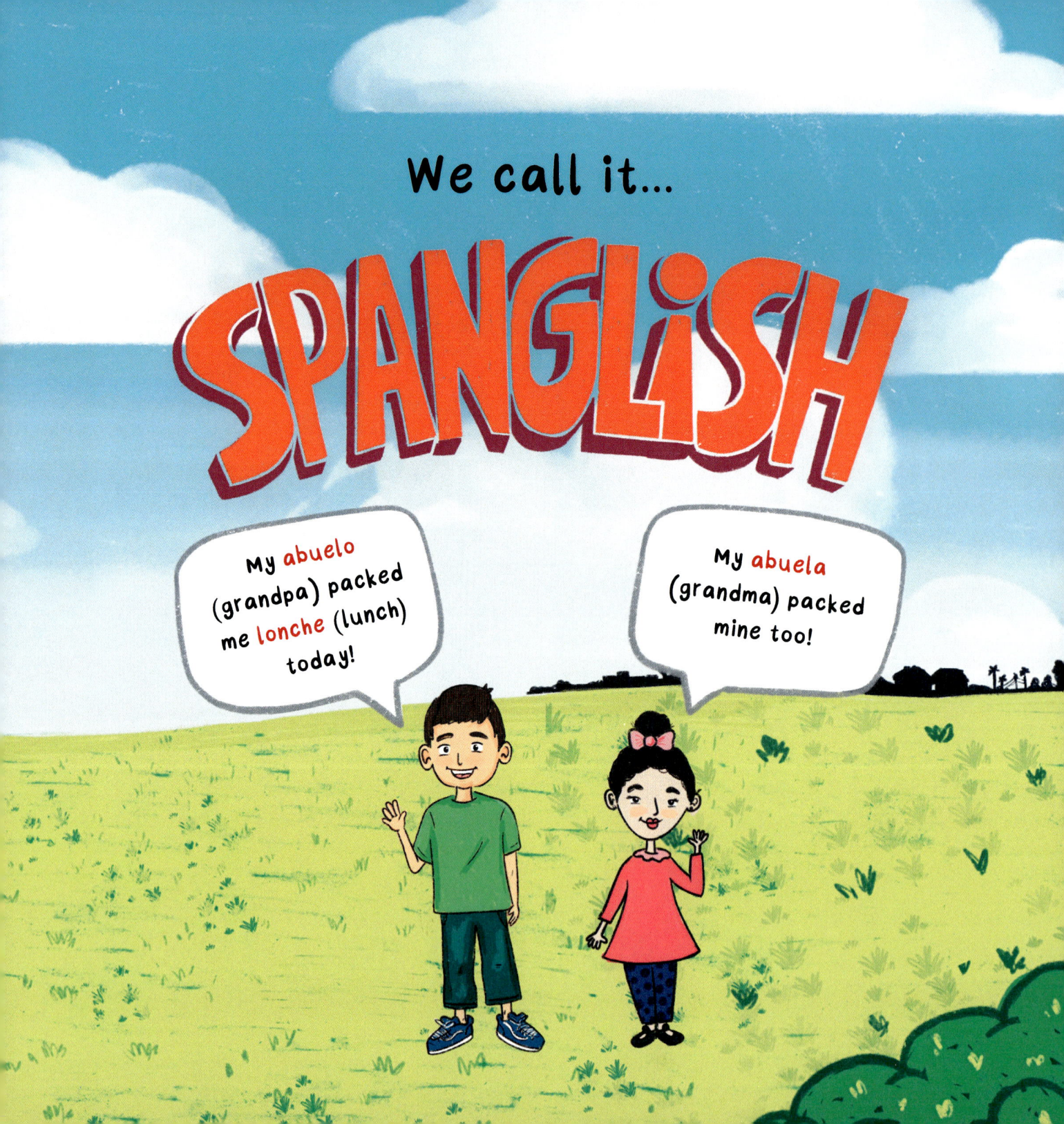

Where I live in South Texas, it is common to be raised bilingually, which means you speak two languages fluently.

It is not unusual to hear people switch back and forth from Spanish to English and English to Spanish. Sometimes we even speak both languages in the same word or sentence.

Yay! We're next! As my grandpa and I approach the window, I see familiar faces waiting to greet us. They know my grandpa and me by name and are always so friendly.

"¡Hola Bienvenidos! ¿Cómo están?" Genaro says.
("Hello! Welcome! How are you all?")

"Hi, Lupita and Genaro!" I say

"Hola. Muy bien, gracias. Gusto en verlos," Grandpa Chavez says.
("Hi. Very good, thank you. It's a pleasure to see you all.")

"What antojitos (cravings) are we in the mood for today?" says Lupita.

"Wow! That looks like a delicious Grape Piccadilly, Leticia! Enjoy!"

"Oh, I will!" as she says goodbye to me with her raspa in her hand and her Grandma Lela's hand in the other.

I love piccadillys, but I am not in the mood for tangy and sweet today. I am going to stick to my rainbow raspa!

As I am about to ask my grandpa which raspa he is going to choose, I hear a voice.

"Carlitos! Look what I got!"
To my surprise, it is my best friend, Leticia!

She is at Raspa King with her Abuela Lela (Grandma Lela)!
She shows me her monster-sized cone! Her raspa is a deep purple color.

What flavor do you think it is? Yes! ¡Uva! (Grape)

It's topped with plenty of chopped pepinillos (pickles) and sprinkled with grape Kool-Aid powder. Just looking at the toppings glisten in the sun tantalizes my taste buds!

I look at the menu and see so many options. It's always so hard to choose just one because everything looks delicious.

As my eyes scan the menu, I see you can create your own rainbow raspa.

You can choose up to three flavors on your snow cone and add toppings.

"Cool! That's the one I'll get!" I thought.

I live in a city named McAllen, TX. It is about 30 minutes from the border of México.

Our South Texas weather is known to be really warm, so there is nothing more refreshing than a delicious raspa on a hot, sunny day!

By the time I know it, we arrive at my favorite snow-cone stand – Raspa King! They have the best raspas and are known for their giant creations!

It is no surprise that there is a long line of customers just as eager as I am to order one of their treats!

Chamoy is a Mexican candy that can be sweet or spicy.
It is a mix of fruit, spices, chiles, dried hibiscus, and sugar.

¡CHAMOY!

Chamoy can be used as a topping or dipping sauce on fruit, chips, raspas, and just about anything you can think of.

Just the thought of it makes my mouth water!

As I hop in his car, Grandpa Chávez says to me,

"Hola Carlitos. ¿Cómo te fue en la escuela hoy?"
("Hello Carlitos. How was school today?")

"Muy bien, Abuelito. ¡Gracias!"
("Very good, Grandpa. Thank you!")

I push open the silver double doors and smile from ear to ear as I see my abuelito (grandpa) parked first in line.

He always arrives early so he can be the first car in the pick-up line.

The school bell rings, and Mrs. Contreras says, "Have a great weekend, Class. You are dismissed!"

I put on my backpack and rush down the hallway while being careful not to bump into any students.

In my family and where I live in South Texas, we call snow cones RASPAS. They come in a variety of bright colors, crazy flavors, and have some of the most mouthwatering toppings you can think of!

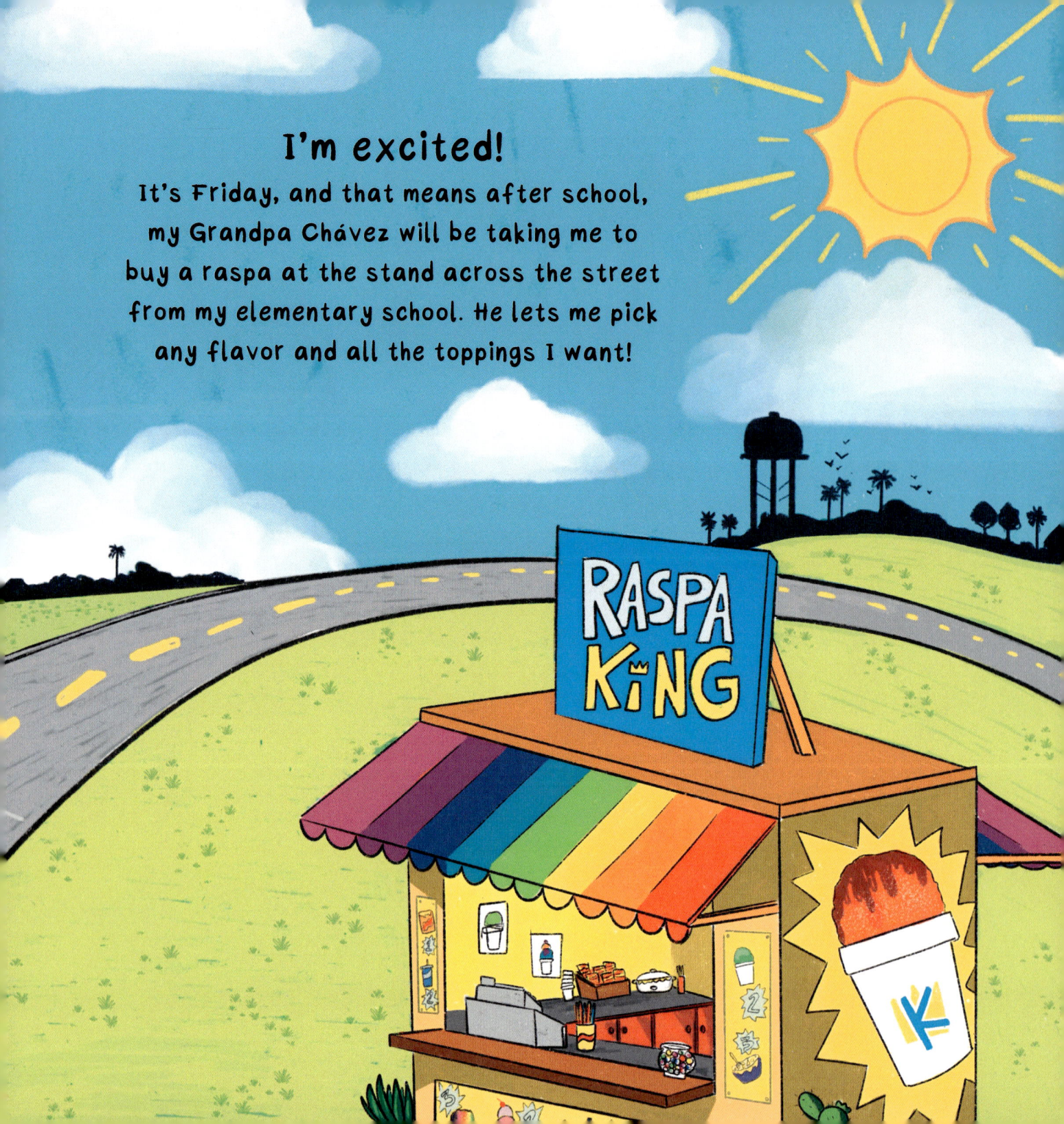

I'm excited!
It's Friday, and that means after school, my Grandpa Chávez will be taking me to buy a raspa at the stand across the street from my elementary school. He lets me pick any flavor and all the toppings I want!

"Thank you so much, Abuelito (Grandpa),"
I say as we walk to the colorful picnic tables to sit down and relish our delicious Mexican treats.

"De nada, Mijo" ("You're welcome, My Son.")
my abuelo says.

RASPAS CON MI GRANDPA SPAN(GL)ISH GLOSSARY

- **Raspa** / Snow cone

Also known as:
- **Raspada or Raspado** (Argentina, Ecuador, Honduras, Mexico, Nicaragua, and Panama)
- **Raspao** (Colombia, Panama, Venezuela (some areas)
- **Raspadilla** (Peru)

A
- **Abuelo** / Abuelito (said with love) / Grandpa
- **Abuela** / Abuelita (said with love) / Grandma
- **Almuerzo** / Lunch
- **Amor** / Love
- **Antojo** / Craving
- **Antojito** / Appetizer

B
- **Bien** / Good / Well
- **Bienvenidos** / Welcome

C
- **¿Cómo están?** / How are you all?

D
- **De Nada** / You're welcome

E
- **Escuela** / School
- **Especialmente** / Especially

G
- **Gracias** / Thank you

H
- **Hola** / Hello

L
- **Listo** / Ready
- **Lonche** (Spanglish for Lunch)

M
- **Mija o Mi + hija** / my daughter
- **Mijo o Mi + hijo** / my son

P
- **Pepinos o Pepinillos** / Pickles

S
- **Sabor** / Flavor
- **Si** / Yes

U
- **Uva** / Grape

MEET THE REAL GRANDPA CHÁVEZ

This is Feliberto. He is remembered for being a fun, loving, and humorous grandpa that loved his wife, children, and grandchildren deeply. He loved having breakfast at Lee's Pharmacy in McAllen, TX, with his children and long-time friends. He enjoyed watching western movies, listening to music, cracking jokes, exercising, shopping, studying geography, writing poetry, painting, and reading his Bible.
He really was always the first car in the pick-up line!

AUTHOR BIO

Eliza Garza is a speaker and entrepreneur in South Texas where she owns and operates a Mexican street eats business that specializes in raspas! Eliza is passionate about her Hispanic heritage and is proud to integrate it into the many facets of her life. She believes that part of a child's pathway to empowerment and authenticity is understanding, identifying, and embracing their culture at a young age.

Eliza is the founder of Adventure in a Cup, a program that provides children with the opportunity to learn the principles of entrepreneurship, financial literacy, and goal setting by practicing with their own raspa stand for a day. Eliza enjoys spending time with her family, which includes her spoiled poodle named Brinkley, being an active member of her community, and hosting collaborative and empowering events in her spare time.

Bookings:

Book Eliza M. Garza for your next school function, book fair, conference, or corporate event. E-mail: authorelizamgarza@gmail.com for more information.

Edna Galván is a freelance graphic designer and illustrator originally from Tampico Tams. Mexico, but currently living in McAllen Tx. Since a young age, she enjoys drawing and creating new ideas everyday. In addition to art, she enjoys outside activities and a good cup of coffee.

JOIN OUR SUBSCRIBER LIST!

Get a FREE Raspas Con Mi Grandpa coloring sheet when you sign up! Be the first to know about new book launches, book signings, special promotions, sales, giveaways, and more!

  @authorelizamgarza

  @authorelizamg

Made in the USA
Coppell, TX
03 March 2026